The lamb lay weakly in the stra~~w, sh~~

When Father came to see th~~...~~ head. "That one won't make ~~...~~

Hannah looked down at ~~...~~ and sad. Its eyes seemed to b~~...~~ ~~...~~ *~~...~~* ber. "Maybe I could feed it," she said.

For a moment, Father did not answer. "It might take cow's milk," he said slowly. "But it would need to be fed every hour or two. All night long. And even then it is likely to sicken and die." Again he shook his head.

"I can do it," Hannah said eagerly. "Please, Father. Let me try."

Father brought a pail full of Bessie's warm milk and an old bit of rag. "See if it will suck on this," he said.

Hannah sat on the straw beside the black lamb. It was so weak, it could hardly lift up its head. She dipped the rag into the milk, then held it next to the baby's nose. The lamb didn't seem to know what to do. Very carefully she opened its mouth and pushed the end of the rag inside.

The lamb spluttered and spit it out.

"Come on," she coaxed. "Just taste it."

The Pioneer Daughters series
by Jean Van Leeuwen

Hannah of Fairfield
Hannah's Helping Hands
Hannah's Winter of Hope

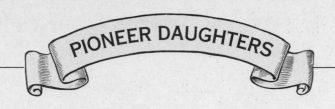

PIONEER DAUGHTERS

Hannah of Fairfield

JEAN VAN LEEUWEN

PICTURES BY DONNA DIAMOND

PUFFIN BOOKS

To the Perley family, my New England ancestors
—J.V.L.

PUFFIN BOOKS
Published by the Penguin Group
Penguin Putnam Books for Young Readers,
345 Hudson Street, New York, New York 10014, U.S.A.
Penguin Books Ltd, 27 Wrights Lane, London W8 5TZ, England
Penguin Books Australia Ltd, Ringwood, Victoria, Australia
Penguin Books Canada Ltd, 10 Alcorn Avenue, Toronto, Ontario, Canada M4V 3B2
Penguin Books (N.Z.) Ltd, 182-190 Wairau Road, Auckland 10, New Zealand

Penguin Books Ltd, Registered Offices: Harmondsworth, Middlesex, England

First published in the United States of America by Dial Books for Young Readers,
a division of Penguin Putnam Inc., 1999
Published by Puffin Books,
a division of Penguin Putnam Books for Young Readers, 2000

9 10 8

THE LIBRARY OF CONGRESS HAS CATALOGED THE DIAL EDITION AS FOLLOWS:
Van Leeuwen, Jean.
Hannah of Fairfield / by Jean Van Leeuwen ;
pictures by Donna Diamond.—1st ed.
p. cm.
Summary: For almost-nine-year-old Hannah Perley of Fairfield, Connecticut, growing
up means facing new challenges, both great and small—from saving the life
of a baby lamb to helping the family prepare to send her brother Ben to
join the colonial soldiers in the American Revolutionary War.
ISBN 0-8037-2335-0
1. United States—History—Revolution, 1775-1783—Juvenile fiction. [1. United
States—History—Revolution, 1775-1783—Fiction. 2. Fathers and sons—Fiction.
3. Family life—Fiction.]
PZ7.V3273Han 1999 [Fic]—DC21 98-7947 CIP AC

Puffin Books ISBN 0-14-130499-5

Printed in the United States of America
Book design by Stefanie Rosenfeld

RL: 2.3

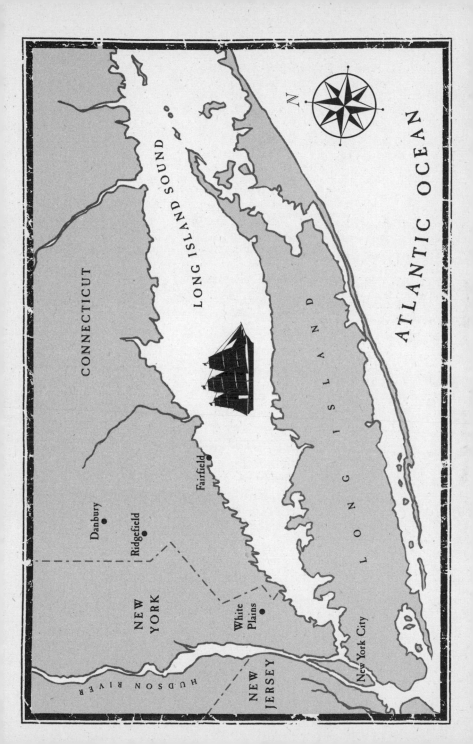

Chapter 1

Right now, thought Hannah, the first lambs of the season were about to be born. Tiny lambs with sweet, round faces. Frisky lambs kicking up their heels in the spring sunshine. She could hardly wait to see them!

But she would have to wait. Hannah pushed out her lower lip. It wasn't fair. Father and her brother Ben got to watch the lambs being born. Sometimes they even slept in the barn to make sure the mothers and babies were all right. But not Hannah.

"That is men's work, not women's work," her mother always said.

Women's work. Hannah looked down at

the mitten she was knitting. Oh, dear. It was all lopsided. And she had hoped to finish it tonight. Then Ben would have a new pair when he went out to chop wood tomorrow.

Could she have dropped a stitch? By the dim light of the fire she began to count. Twenty-five, twenty-six, twenty-seven . . .

"Josiah Plummer has joined the army," Ben said. He was sitting on the stool farthest from the fire, whittling clothespins for Mother. He put down his knife.

"Father," he said quietly, "I want to go too."

The soft hum of her sister Rebecca's spinning wheel stopped. The two younger boys, Jemmy and Jonathan, were suddenly quiet. Even Mother, whose busy needle never stopped, paused in her darning.

Everyone looked at Father.

For a moment there was no sound but the pop and crackle of the fire. Then Father set down his Bible. His long, lean face looked stern as he shook his head. "No," he said. "I cannot allow it."

"But, Father!" Ben jumped up, sending clothespins clattering to the floor. "You know men are needed to fight the British. General Washington has called on Connecticut for more soldiers."

"Men," repeated Father calmly. He was always calm, and usually so gentle. But when he made up his mind, it was made up to stay. "Not boys of fifteen. Boys of fifteen are needed on farms to raise grain to feed the army."

"I will be sixteen by summer," argued Ben. He paced up and down in front of the fire, his face red as the burning coals. "Ebenezer Reed was only fourteen when he ran off to fight. And Josiah just turned sixteen."

Keep your temper, Ben, thought Hannah. She looked up to her oldest brother more than anyone. He was so tall and handsome, with his dark curls and teasing grin. And he could do anything, from plowing a straight row to shooting a pigeon out of a tree to whittling a whistle for five-year-old Jonathan. He felt so strongly about things though that sometimes he spoke out of turn.

"You are too young," Father said firmly. "I cannot do without you on the farm. And have you forgotten about the clock-making trade?"

For almost a year Ben had been an apprentice in Father's shop, building wooden cases for Father's tall clocks. And learning to make the brass insides too.

Ben turned to face him, his eyes flashing.

"How can I sit here making clocks when our country is fighting for its freedom?"

Ben, thought Hannah, you have gone too far this time. No one spoke to Father like that. It was not respectful.

All at once Mother was on her feet, gathering up her sewing. "Come, children," she said. "Time for bed."

Jemmy and Jonathan hurried off to their cold bedchamber. Rebecca wrapped a brick from the fireplace in a scrap of blanket to use as a bedwarmer. Hannah picked up a candlestick to light the way upstairs.

She looked again at her knitting. In the brighter light she could see the mitten's odd, lumpy shape. And yes, there it was. A hole right next to the thumb. What a bother! Now she would have to take out all those rows of stitches. Ben would not have his new mittens tomorrow.

Mother was looking too. "Oh, my," she said, shaking her head. "Never mind, Hannah. We will put it to rights in the morning."

Father and Ben still sat by the fire, quiet now. Father had picked up his Bible again. Ben was staring at the floor.

"Will you check for lambs before you go to bed?" Hannah asked him.

But Ben did not seem to hear.

Upstairs, in the high feather bed she shared with Rebecca, Hannah tried to go to sleep. But she couldn't get warm. The brick didn't really take the chill out of the cold sheets. And she couldn't seem to get comfortable either. In her mind she kept hearing Father's and Ben's voices.

"Go to sleep, Hannah," murmured Rebecca drowsily.

Then Hannah realized that she *was* hearing Father's and Ben's voices. They were arguing again.

A shiver went down Hannah's spine. What if Ben did not back down? What if he ran off to join the army like Ebenezer Reed?

Hannah moved closer to her sister's warm back. Lambs, she thought. Think about lambs. Funny, silly, dear little lambs. In a moment Rebecca's deep breathing said she was asleep. Hannah felt herself drifting off too.

Suddenly Father's voice came up through the floorboards.

"You don't know, Son, what a terrible thing war is."

Lambs, Hannah said to herself. But when she closed her eyes, she could no longer see their sweet, woolly faces.

All she could see was marching soldiers.

Chapter 2

In the morning Ben found the first lamb half-buried in hay next to its mother. And then two more. Hannah ran out to the barn before breakfast to see them.

"They're beautiful!" she exclaimed.

The lambs were standing on wobbly legs, nuzzling their mothers. It was amazing. These babies were just a few hours old. And already they were on their feet and looking around for their first meal. What did they think of this new world they found themselves in?

Hannah wished she could stay and watch all morning, but she had to help with breakfast. And after that it was time to work on her knitting.

In the daylight the mitten looked even worse. Like the work of a five-year-old, not someone soon to be nine. Patiently Mother took it out all the way to the thumb.

"You must pay attention to your stitches, Hannah," she said as she handed back the mitten.

That was the problem, Hannah knew. Knitting was so much the same. Put the long needle in, wind the wool around it, take off the stitch. Do it all again. After a while she couldn't help it. Her mind wandered away.

"I will try," said Hannah. She did want to finish Ben's mitten. And besides, she hated it when Mother looked at her the way she was now. Mother's eyes were so serious, and a tiny frown puckered her forehead.

Mother never looked at Rebecca that way.

"You need to work harder at your needle-work," she said.

Mother was disappointed in her. It wasn't just her knitting. Hannah had barely started her

sampler, a piece of cloth that showed how many different stitches you could do. Rebecca had finished hers when she was seven. And Hannah's friend Betsy Spooner was already halfway along. Mother had told Hannah how important it was for a girl to be able to hem and darn and turn a neat seam. But working those tiny stitches was so hard, and she was always pricking her finger.

Hannah straightened her shoulders.

"I will," she promised. She would pay more attention. Her mind would not wander. And she would finish Ben's mitten today.

It was a good day for needlework. A light rain pattered on the windows. Perhaps it would wash away the last of the March snow. Father had taken the younger boys with him to Mr. Spooner's store. Ben was at the woodlot down the road. Mother and Rebecca were working, as they had almost all winter, on tents for General Washington's army. Rebecca did the spinning, on the small flax wheel. Mother did the weaving, on the great square loom upstairs.

But this morning Mother was not at her loom. She sat winding the thread into long loops called skeins. It was quiet in the room. The only sounds were the *click* of Hannah's needles, the *whirr-sigh* of the spinning wheel, and the *tock-tock* of the tall clock in the corner. It was the first one Father had ever made.

There was something peaceful about needlework, Hannah had to admit. Maybe that was why Mother liked it so much. As she worked, her face wore the smallest smile, one she didn't even know she was smiling.

"By the end of the month," Mother said, "I believe we will have finished one hundred and eighty yards."

One hundred and eighty yards of tent cloth. That would make a lot of tents, Hannah thought. And then there were all the wool blankets and stockings and mittens that Mother and Rebecca had finished. Not one was for the family. Except for Hannah's mittens for Ben, the Perley family was making do with what they had. Everything they made was for General Washington's army.

It was the same with Father. He spent less time at his clock-making now and more in the fields, growing extra wheat and corn to feed the soldiers. Their neighbors were all planting more too. The town of Fairfield was proud of the way it was helping fight the British.

All of this had been going on almost as long as Hannah could remember. Ever since the April day two years ago, in 1775, when Ben had come running home to tell what he had seen on the village green.

"A horseman came galloping up to Thaddeus Burr's house," he told them breathlessly, "and handed him a scroll. You should have seen his horse, dripping and puffing. He'd been riding three days from Boston to spread news of the fighting. Rode so hard the first day, his horse fell down dead."

The fighting was at Lexington and Concord in Massachusetts. There, Ben said, British troops had fired on a small group of men.

Hannah had been full of questions. What was the fighting about? she asked. Why were we fighting the British? Weren't we British too?

Father had explained.

"You're right," he said, smiling at her. "These lands were settled by Englishmen. But England has treated its American colonies badly. Always wanting more taxes, even on tea. That is why we don't drink it anymore. And sending soldiers to watch over us. This fighting was bound to come."

As soon as the tired horseman rode off to New York that April day, men began to gather on the village green. A few days later, nearly fifty soldiers marched off to Boston. Ben watched them go. Hannah saw him pull himself up tall, his feet stepping to the beat of the drums. From that moment on, Ben had longed to be one of them, a Patriot fighting against the British.

Father was such a strong Patriot himself.

Why, Hannah wondered now, was he so set against Ben's going?

". . . And with Hannah's help," Mother said, "we will be able to do even more."

Oh, dear. Hannah's mind had wandered. Had she ruined her knitting again? She peered down at the mitten. No more mistakes that she could see. She breathed a sigh of relief. But Mother was looking at her.

"I've been thinking it is time for you to help with the spinning," she said.

Hannah's heart sank. That was something else she wasn't good at. She had tried. But somehow she couldn't get the feel of it.

"Don't frown so, Hannah." Rebecca smiled at her. "I will help you."

Sometimes it was hard to remember that her sister was just thirteen. Already she seemed like a grown woman. And she looked just like Mother, small and neat with quick, gray eyes and pale yellow hair. Hair the color of flax. Hannah's hair was the color of mud.

"It's very simple really," said Rebecca. She

showed Hannah again how to press the foot treadle, the pedal that started the wheel spinning. How to wet her fingers in the water bowl. How, with her left hand, to draw out the fibers from the bundle of flax tied to the wheel. And, with her right hand, smooth it as it spun into thread.

"Slow down the wheel a little," suggested Mother.

"And don't let the flax twist too tight," added Rebecca.

After watching a few minutes, they left her. Hannah could hear the squeak of chairs and the thump of the loom in the room above her head.

Pay attention. Keep the wheel going. She could do this, Hannah thought. Draw out the fibers with one hand. At the same time, smooth with the other.

At the same time. That was the problem. Hannah's hands and feet seemed to belong to two different people. When she thought about the flax between her fingers, her foot stopped rocking. And when she thought about her treadling, the flax twisted too tight.

Hannah stopped the wheel. She looked at the thread Rebecca had spun, so smooth and fine. And then at her own. Hers was all lumps and bumps.

Tears filled her eyes. She sat very still. No sounds came now from upstairs. All she could hear was the *tock-tock* of Father's clock.

"You can't do it," it seemed to say. "You can't do it."

Chapter 3

Finally she had escaped. Away from the spinning wheel that made her feel so clumsy. To the barn.

Hannah loved everything about the barn. Its smells, of sweet hay and old wood and animals all mixed together. Its sounds, the little creaks and rustles and stamping of feet. And, most of all, the animals. There was Ned, the big chestnut horse, and the two cows, Hattie and old Bessie, and, of course, the sheep.

It was late afternoon, the best time of day in the barn. The animals were snug and settled in their stalls. Jemmy sat on a stool milking Bessie, while little Jonathan stood on tiptoe to pat her nose.

The old cow stood still while the milk *splish-splashed* into the pail.

"Good old Bessie," Hannah said, stroking her neck. "You are as patient as the day is long." Her mother always said that. "And sweet as maple sugar."

The cow's ear flicked in answer.

"More like bee's honey," said a deep voice. It seemed to be coming from inside Bessie's chest.

Hannah looked up, startled, to see Jemmy's grinning face.

"Ha! I caught you!" He was laughing so hard, he fell off the stool. "You thought old Bessie was answering, didn't you?"

Hannah felt herself turning pink. "I never did. I knew it was you."

Jemmy climbed back onto his stool. His straw-colored hair had bits of hay stuck all over it. "You really talk to cows?" he said, shaking his head.

Hannah didn't answer. Jemmy always acted as if he knew everything, just because he was a year older, and a boy besides.

Why was it, Hannah wondered, as she often had before, that boys got all the good chores, like milking and herding sheep and chopping wood? Even little Jonathan gathered the warm eggs from the henhouse each morning. Girls had to be inside, knitting and sewing and spinning. Sitting still. Hannah hated sitting still.

She felt Jonathan's mouth next to her ear.

"I talk to Ned," he whispered. Jonathan loved horses. He was always climbing up on the rail of Ned's stall to pet him. "And do you know what?" His wide brown eyes were serious.

"What?" she whispered in his ear.

"Sometimes he talks back."

Hannah smiled at him. "Come on," she said, taking his small hand in hers. "Let's go see the lambs."

The three babies and their mothers were in a corner stall apart from the other sheep.

"Look," said Jonathan. "They're awake!"

Sometimes the new lambs just dozed in the straw. But these babies were on their feet. Already they seemed stronger than they had this morning. They looked as if they wanted to play.

They took little jumps, forward, backward, and sideways. They fell down. Then they were up on their fuzzy, gray legs again. Their mothers lay in the straw, quietly chewing. Silly children, they seemed to be thinking.

Hannah had to smile. If she ever felt sad, all she had to do was watch the lambs, with their sweet faces and foolish-looking tails, playing.

Jonathan tugged at her sleeve. "Look at the biggest one," he said.

One lamb had climbed on a pile of hay in the corner. For a moment it stood there, like the king of the mountain. *"Baa,"* it bleated in its baby voice.

"That one is my favorite," said Jonathan. "Do you think I could name it?"

Hannah nodded. "Father wouldn't mind."

Jonathan thought for a minute, his face screwed up in a frown.

"King," he said.

"That," said Hannah, "is a perfect name."

They watched until, all at once, the three lambs seemed to wear themselves out. They curled up next to their mothers in the straw.

Hannah was still smiling as she walked out of the barn.

"No food for you," she told the geese, who crowded around her feet. They always thought everyone had corn for them. They scolded her, pecking at the ground, when they saw her hands were empty.

As she shooed them away, she noticed someone out in the field behind the house. No, two people. Father and Ben, she thought.

"Ben!" she called. "I've nearly finished your mitten."

But he was too far away to hear. He had Father's musket on his shoulder. Had he been hunting rabbits?

The other person had a gun too. That was not Father. It was Ben's friend Daniel Wakefield, who lived on the next farm. And they were not hunting. They were marching.

Marching like soldiers.

Oh, Ben. Hannah let out a breath. After everything Father had said, Ben had not given up on being a soldier. Not only was he still thinking about it, he was drilling. Getting ready.

Hannah's heart sank all the way down to her muddy shoes. This could only mean one thing.

Ben was going to run away and join General Washington's army.

Chapter 4

S he would talk to Ben. She would ask him what he was going to do.

Hannah always had so many questions. And Ben never seemed to mind answering them. Questions about shearing the sheep or whittling an axe handle or loading Father's musket. Girls weren't supposed to be curious about axes and guns. But Hannah was.

Ben liked to show her things too. Like how he chose just the right tree to make a case for a tall clock. How he split a fat log into boards. How he fit those boards together, straight as could be, until he'd made a case fine enough to hold one of Father's brass clock movements.

Hannah loved to watch him work in the little clock-making shop near the barn.

That was the place to go to talk to Ben.

"Hello, Goosey," he greeted her. That was Ben's name for Hannah because, he said, she was always pecking into things. But he didn't grin as he usually did. And he didn't stop his hammering on a brass clock dial.

Hannah watched for a few minutes. She didn't quite know how to ask the question on her mind. Finally Ben set down his hammer.

"Um—do you like your mittens?" she asked.

"They fit just right," he said. "There's only one thing. Where are all the dropped stitches?" Now he flashed her that teasing grin.

"I fixed them," she answered. Hannah hesitated. Then she added, "You can wear them the next time you and Daniel go hunting rabbits."

"Rabbits?" Ben looked puzzled.

"Was that what you were doing out in the field yesterday?"

Ben looked down at the workbench. He

didn't answer. That was strange. Ben always answered her questions.

"No," he mumbled finally. But that was all. He picked up his hammer and began pounding once more. And this time he didn't stop to rest. After a while Hannah gave up and wandered away.

She tried again a few days later.

They were in the barn, watching the newest lambs, which had just been born. They were twins, one black and one white. The babies were trying to stand up, but their little legs kept collapsing under them.

"Ma-a," cried the black one, as if asking its mother for help.

"Baa-aa," answered the mother sheep. Keep trying, she seemed to say.

After a few more tries both lambs were standing and taking a few shaky steps. The white one found its mother's udder. It began to nurse.

Ben leaned over the stall, smiling as he

watched. "It's amazing," he said. "They always know just what to do."

This was her chance, Hannah realized.

"Ben," she blurted out, "are you going to join the army?"

It wasn't the way she had planned to say it. But there it was. The question hung in the air, seeming to echo in the quiet of the barn.

Ben's back stiffened. His smile faded. Slowly he shook his head.

"I don't know yet, Goosey," he said softly.

What did that mean? Had he been arguing with Father again? Had he and Daniel talked about running away? Hannah wanted to shout out questions. But something stopped her. Something in his eyes and the way his jaw was set made him seem different. Not the boy she knew so well. More like a man.

Now he was frowning at the mother sheep and her babies. "It looks as if we have trouble," he said.

The black lamb was trying to nurse along

with the white one. But the mother moved away. The baby tried again. Suddenly the mother turned and pushed the black lamb so hard with her head that it fell down.

"*M-m-m-a,*" cried the baby, sprawled in the straw.

Sometimes, Ben had told Hannah, a mother sheep didn't seem to understand that a lamb belonged to her. Especially if she was a mother for the first time. She refused to feed it. If the mother didn't feed it, the lamb could die.

"Please, mother sheep," whispered Hannah, "take care of your baby."

But twice more the mother sheep knocked over the black lamb. Finally it just lay weakly in the straw, shaking.

When Father came to see the new lambs, he shook his head. "That one won't make it," he said.

Hannah looked down at the black lamb, so helpless and sad. Its eyes seemed to be pleading with her. "Maybe I could feed it," she said.

For a moment Father did not answer. "It

might take cow's milk," he said slowly. "But it would need to be fed every hour or two. All night long. And even then it is likely to sicken and die." Again he shook his head.

"I can do it," Hannah said eagerly. "Please, Father. Let me try."

Father looked at her for a long moment. "Are you sure? It will be difficult. And the chances of saving this lamb are small."

"I know." Hannah looked back, her eyes pleading like the lamb's.

"All right then."

Father brought a pail full of Bessie's warm milk and an old bit of rag. "See if it will suck on this," he said.

Hannah sat on the straw beside the black lamb. It was so weak, it could hardly lift up its head. She dipped the rag into the milk, then held it next to the baby's nose. The lamb didn't seem to know what to do. Very carefully she opened its mouth and pushed the end of the rag inside.

The lamb spluttered and spit it out.

"It's all right, baby," she said softly, stroking its head.

What else could she try?

Hannah thought for a minute. She put a drop of milk on her finger, then brought it up to the lamb's mouth. "Come on," she coaxed. "Just taste it."

She felt a tiny nibble at her finger.

Hannah smiled. "See how good it is?"

After a few more drops she tried the rag again. This time the lamb seemed to understand. It pulled at the rag, as if it were nursing from its mother. Then, suddenly, its eyes closed and it was asleep.

Hannah watched its woolly side go up and down. Up and down. Yes, it was breathing.

Father's long shadow fell over the stall. "Well," he said, "you seem to have made a start."

"Good work, Goosey." Ben was grinning broadly. "I'll bring you some supper. And a blanket."

A little later he came back with a slab of

brown bread, a piece of cheese, and a mug of cider. Two blankets and a lantern. And Jonathan.

"I could stay too," said Jonathan, bouncing with excitement. "Sometimes I'm awake a long time in the night. I could wake you up if you fall asleep."

"Sorry, Half-a-Pint-Full." Ben swooped Jonathan up onto his shoulders. "Come on," he said. "I'll give you a horseback ride."

"But what if Hannah falls asleep?" Jonathan's dark eyes were worried.

"I won't," said Hannah. "I promise."

Jonathan leaned down, his hands clutching Ben's curls. "Good night, Hannah. Good night, lamb. Did you give it a name?"

Hannah shook her head. She hadn't thought of naming it. Not if it might die. That seemed like bad luck.

"I'll think about it while I am staying awake," she said.

After Ben and Jonathan left, Hannah ate her

bread and cheese, washing them down with cider. Then she spread out one of the blankets. She lifted the sleeping lamb onto her lap. It felt soft as flannel, limp and warm.

Could she really stay awake all night? she wondered.

The lamb needed her. And Father had let her do this. She had to.

Through the long night the lamb woke and sucked and fell asleep again. Hannah kept watching it. Did it seem a little stronger? Was it breathing all right? She couldn't tell. But it was still alive. That was good.

She struggled to stay awake. Many times she felt her eyelids growing heavy. Trying to close. Closing. She jerked herself upright. She thought of names. Blackie? Midnight? Or a flower name. Daisy? No, that wasn't right.

She watched the lantern flicker and smoke as the candle burned low. Smoke, she thought sleepily. Don't forget, smoke. Why was that important?

Finally the candle sputtered out. The blackness of the barn was just melting into gray when her eyes closed. And this time they wouldn't open.

The rooster woke her, proudly telling of the new day. Bright sunshine was streaming into the barn. And Jonathan was tugging at her foot.

The lamb still slept, sprawled across her chest. She could feel its breathing mixed up with her own.

Hannah looked up into Jonathan's questioning face.

"It's alive," she said. "And its name is Smoke."

Chapter 5

Smoke followed Hannah everywhere.

"I believe she thinks you are her mother." Ben laughed.

The little black lamb was healthy and frisky. Hannah kept feeding her, with Ben's help. As the days went by, it seemed sure she was going to survive. Soon she was playing with King and the other lambs.

"Good job, Daughter," was all Father had said that morning when Jonathan ran to tell him the lamb was alive. Father wasn't much for compliments. But Hannah could see in his eyes that he was proud of her.

Hannah felt proud too. And amazed. She had actually saved a life.

Mother kept telling her that she reminded her of her own mother, whose name had been Hannah too. "Do you remember her?" she asked.

Hannah wasn't sure. Grandmother Pritchard had died when Hannah was just three. But she thought she remembered someone with a round, smiling face. Someone who always smelled of peppermint.

"She was a midwife," Mother told her. "She delivered babies, but she also treated other illnesses. She had her own medicines, and many folks thought they were better than those of the old doctor in town. And whenever she was sent for, she always went. I remember stormy nights when the roads were blocked with snow. She would strap on her snowshoes and walk ten miles to deliver a baby. 'Tell them I will be there,' she always said."

Mother smiled at the memory.

For the next few days Hannah carried around a picture inside her head. Of her small, round grandmother walking over snowdrifts to save a life.

In Fairfield the snow had melted and the mud dried up. The sun felt warm now on Hannah's bare head. New leaves were popping out on the trees. The fields were fresh-turned brown and full of promise. Soon sprouts of corn and flax and buckwheat would be coming up. Yes, spring had finally arrived.

One bright April morning the family set out for church. They walked across the village green as the church bell rang out its call to worship.

Ben was quiet. He looked worn out from long hours of plowing. And Hannah could tell that things were still not right between him and Father. They barely spoke to each other. Still, she had heard no more arguments. Maybe, then, it was settled. He was staying on the farm.

"Good morning, Timothy." Father nodded to Daniel's father.

"Good morning, Nathaniel."

Something seemed different about Mr. Wakefield this morning. His broad face looked unusually serious, Hannah thought. But that was not all. He was carrying his musket.

He wasn't the only one. So was Jeremiah Turner, the blacksmith. And General Silliman, the head of the militia, the soldiers who guarded the town. Everywhere she looked, she saw men carrying guns. Guns to church! Hannah felt her heart skip. What was wrong?

All through the long service she wondered. She tried to listen to Reverend Eliot's sermon. But her thoughts kept wandering.

Ever since last fall when the British army had captured New York City, their ships had been making raids on towns like Fairfield. They would come in the night, stealing cattle or burning mills. Fairfield had tried to defend itself. There was the fort overlooking the harbor at Black Rock. And militia soldiers stood guard at night, watching for enemy boats. But still the raids on towns along the shore continued. Just last month two more cannons had been added to the fort.

Had there been another raid? Or had ships been sighted on Long Island Sound? Hannah sighed. She would have to wait to find out.

Her mother glanced over at her, frowning. She knew what that meant. *Stop fidgeting. Listen to the sermon. Like Rebecca.* Her sister sat perfectly still, her eyes on the minister's face. And even little Jonathan was amazingly good, his feet only once in a while kicking the seat in front of him.

But not Jemmy. A constant buzz came from the balcony, where the older boys and slaves and Indians sat. Hannah couldn't see what they were doing. But if there was any mischief up there, Jemmy would be in the middle of it.

The deacon turned the hourglass. Again. Two hours, and still the minister showed no sign of finishing his sermon. Hannah's feet were numb. They hadn't brought the footwarmer today, as they did in winter. Even though it was warm outside, the unheated church was cold and damp.

"Jemmy Perley, you stop that!"

A loud whisper came from the balcony. Loud enough for everyone to hear. Then some shuffling, and a couple of sharp thumps.

Hannah looked over at Mother and Father. They were both staring straight ahead. Perhaps Father hadn't heard. In church he always seemed far away. But a bright spot of pink burned on Mother's cheek.

Watch out, Jemmy. You are in trouble now, thought Hannah.

When the service finally ended, Jemmy was nowhere to be seen.

"He is hiding out," Ben said. "Hoping Mother won't remember by the time we get home."

"What did he do?" Hannah asked, curious.

"Tickled Billy Partridge's neck with a straw."

In spite of herself, Hannah had to smile. Billy Partridge was a big, slow lump of a boy. It would take a lot of tickling to make him speak out in church.

Then she remembered. The guns.

"Why have so many men brought guns to church?" she asked Ben.

"I don't know," Ben answered. "But I will find out."

He joined a group of men near the church steps. Hannah had to stay with Mother. It wasn't fair. Why couldn't she find out as easily as Ben?

Mother was busy talking with Mrs. Wakefield and Mrs. Spooner. Hannah moved a few steps away from the circle of women. She strained her ears. But still she couldn't make out what the men were saying.

She had an idea. She took out her handkerchief and dropped it into the grass. She looked to see if anyone was watching. Then she kicked the handkerchief toward the steps. Just as she'd hoped, the breeze carried it almost there.

Quickly she ran to pick it up. As she bent down, she listened carefully.

"General Silliman has had a warning," she heard someone say.

"The enemy is gathering in New York. . . ."

". . .They plan to destroy army supplies in Danbury and other parts."

So that was why men were carrying guns on a Sunday. Danbury was a town close by. If the British came, what might happen to Fairfield?

Hannah hurried back to stand next to Mother. The women were not talking of danger. They were talking about tents for the soldiers.

"We must plan a spinning bee," Mother was saying.

"Oh, yes," Mrs. Wakefield agreed. "You can bring your wheels to my house, and we will sit out in the garden and spin."

"As soon as the plowing and planting are finished," said Mrs. Spooner.

Did they seem worried too? Were their eyes and smiles a little too bright? Hannah couldn't be sure.

Her friend Betsy Spooner interrupted her thoughts.

"Will you be going to school for the summer term?" she asked.

"I hope so," answered Hannah.

"Oh, so do I!" Betsy's blond curls bounced. "Ask your mother if you can."

Hannah wanted very much to go. She had missed the winter term. She'd been practicing her reading with the Bible, the only book the family owned. And Ben had helped her with her numbers. Still, she longed to learn more. And especially to have more books to read. She had read the Bible three times now.

On the way home she asked Mother, "May I go to school this summer?"

Mother kept looking behind them. She was looking for Jemmy, Hannah knew. He still hadn't come out of hiding.

"I know how much you want to go," she said. "And we want you to. But I don't know if I will be able to spare you. There is the shearing of the sheep next month. And then summer will be busy with the dyeing and spinning. We want to make even more blankets for the soldiers this year."

In the summer the women spun wool for blankets and winter clothes. In the winter they spun flax for summer linen. And most of it now was for the soldiers.

Once, Hannah remembered, Mother had woven pretty new dresses for Rebecca and her. Bright yellow for Rebecca, to go with her hair. And soft blue for Hannah, to match her eyes. The three of them had laughed together as they picked out the colors from the dyed skeins of wool drying in the attic.

She frowned. Blankets for the soldiers. Spinning bees. Father and Ben angry at each other. Guns at church. No school. Everything, it seemed, had been changed by this war.

Mother touched her shoulder. "We'll see," she promised.

Jemmy came home in time for dinner. Of course he would, even if it was only last night's pork and beans that couldn't be warmed up because of the Sabbath. For once he didn't have a word to say.

Father said nothing either, until the meal was over. Then he cleared his throat. "James," he said quietly.

No one ever called Jemmy by his real name. He was in trouble now.

"I will not scold you today, not on the

Lord's Day. But tomorrow we will talk about your disrespect."

Jemmy hung his head. "Yes, sir."

"And tomorrow," said Mother, "I believe I will be able to find a few extra chores for you."

Chapter 6

It was just a few days later when Ben came banging through the kitchen doorway.

"Where is Father?" he asked. His cheeks were red and he was breathing hard, as if he had been running.

"I don't know," said Hannah. "What is wrong?"

Mother poked her head in from the buttery.

Ben struggled to speak. "I was clamming," he said, "with Daniel. We looked out in the water and saw them just offshore."

"Saw what?" Mother's eyes grew wide.

"British ships," answered Ben. "Twenty sails or more."

Hannah's heart suddenly began to pound. Would the British land? Were they going to attack Fairfield? Or would they march on to Danbury?

Messengers soon raced along the roads, spreading the news. Yes, the enemy had landed just west of town. Two thousand of them, it was said. And General Silliman had called out the militia. Soldiers began to gather on the green. Hannah saw William Wakefield, Daniel's older brother, go marching off. But where were the soldiers marching to? No one knew.

Father sat calmly at the table, eating his favorite supper of clam chowder and young dandelion greens.

"We must not panic," he said. "Most likely Danbury is the target, not Fairfield, as that is where our army's supplies are stored. Still, we cannot be sure. We will have to wait to learn more."

Ben had not eaten a single bite of supper. He kept going to the door, looking out and listening. He would sit down, then jump up again.

"Let me find out the latest news," he pleaded with Father. "I will walk down the road just to the tavern. I can take the musket for safety."

"I'll go with him," offered Jemmy, his eyes round with excitement.

Father pushed his soup bowl away. For a moment he stared hard at both boys. When he spoke, his voice was quiet and firm. "No one is leaving this house tonight," he said.

It was a long, restless night. The whole house seemed to be holding its breath, waiting and listening. Father and Ben sat by the fire all night long. Hannah felt as if she would never fall asleep. A dozen times or more she sat straight up in bed, sure she had heard them. The marching feet. The *tat-tat* of drums. But it was all inside her head.

Daniel brought the news early the next morning.

"They marched on toward Danbury," he said. His thin, freckled face was pale, as if he had not slept much either. "Our soldiers are going after them. But they outnumber us, four or five to one."

He and Ben looked at each other. Hannah could guess what that look meant. They wished they were among the soldiers going after them.

Father saw the look too, and frowned. "There is nothing we can do now," he said firmly. "Daniel, you best get home. And Ben, we need to finish planting that north field today."

Ben's eyes locked with Father's. He did not say a word, but some kind of struggle seemed to be going on. For a long minute no one spoke. Then Ben jumped up and ran from the room, knocking over a chair as he went.

For the next three days everyone waited.

It was strange, Hannah thought. They knew fighting was going on nearby. Men might be dying. She remembered Daniel's older brother,

William, quiet and hardworking and kind, marching off down the road. What if he never came back?

But in Fairfield everything seemed so normal. Smoke and the other lambs bounced around the barnyard on their springy little legs. Baby geese were hatching. And there was a new batch of fuzzy kittens in the hayloft.

The chores went on too. Long ago Father had fenced in a square patch behind the house. This was where Mother grew her vegetables. Carrots, onions, cabbage, potatoes. Beets, squash, turnips, pumpkins. And the herbs: parsley, sage, mint, chamomile. And others whose names Hannah couldn't remember.

"I'll help you dig," she offered that first morning. Hannah hoped Mother had forgotten about wanting her to spin. She hadn't said anything about it lately. Hannah liked working in the garden so much better.

"I can use some help," Mother agreed.

It felt good to sink her shovel into the soft,

black earth. And Hannah especially liked dropping in the seeds saved from last fall's harvest.

"I think I will plant some feverfew this year," Mother said as they stopped at the end of a row to rest. "And perhaps some tansy."

"Feverfew?" That was a strange name, Hannah thought.

"Your grandmother always had feverfew in her garden," Mother said. "She brewed it into a tea for headache and fever. And tansy was her cure for a baby's colic. She grew so many herbs for cures. And she gathered wild plants too. I used to go along with her when she picked them. Her simples, she called them. She wrote them all down in a book. Someday I'll show it to you."

Hannah thought of all the wild green things growing in the yard, the fields, the woods. It was amazing to think that each one had a name. And each might be a cure for something.

They dug another row, then rested again.

"Some of your grandmother's cures were

unusual," Mother said, smiling. "I remember one time she was called to the home of the young minister and his wife. This was just a few years back. 'Granny Hannah,' they called her then. She was past seventy. A baby had been born too soon, and the doctor didn't think he could save him. 'But see what Granny Hannah can do,' he said.

"Well, your grandmother bathed the tiny thing in warm goose oil. Then she wrapped him in blankets and set him in a box next to the fire. All night long she sat with him, dipping a feather in milk and dripping it into the baby's mouth. And that baby came through. Some in the church said it was a miracle."

Granny Hannah. Hannah liked that name. And now she had another picture in her head. Of her grandmother sitting next to the fire, dripping milk into the mouth of a newborn baby with a feather. Why, that was almost like feeding a newborn lamb with a rag, she thought.

No word of the British came all that day. Or most of the next. But late in the afternoon Daniel stopped by again.

"Have you heard?" he asked breathlessly. "They say Danbury's been burned. All our supplies destroyed, and houses and barns set afire."

And more news came the third day. There was fighting in Ridgefield, another town nearby. The Patriot forces had set up a roadblock and attacked the British as they marched back to their ships.

"This is madness!" Father exclaimed when he heard it. "We have only about six hundred men to their two thousand."

"But we have General Arnold leading our forces," argued Ben. "Along with General Silliman and General Wooster."

General Benedict Arnold was known for his bravery, Hannah knew. He had captured Fort Ticonderoga in New York two years ago. He was Ben's hero.

But Father just kept shaking his head.

Hannah was helping Mother plant seeds in the garden when they heard the gunfire. At first she thought it was thunder.

She and Mother both stood up to listen.

Again it came, dull and far away. But yes, the sound of guns.

"It's coming from Ridgefield way," Mother said. "The fighting must still be going on over there."

Hannah stood still, a handful of pumpkin seeds in her fist. How strange it felt to be putting seeds into the ground while men were shooting at each other so close by. She should be doing something else. But what?

Mother touched her arm. "It is a terrible thing to think about. I know it is. But the living must go on living." Seeds in her hand, she knelt down again.

After a minute Hannah knelt too, and began dropping pumpkin seeds into the warm, dark earth.

In the end the news was just what Father had feared. There were too many of the British. After a short, fierce battle, they ran over the roadblock at Ridgefield. Then, still chased by the Patriots, they marched back to their ships and sailed away.

Everyone was talking about the burning.

"Thirty-six houses and barns set afire in Danbury," Father told the family the next night. "Barrels of food, grain, medicines, tents—all destroyed."

"William says more houses and a mill were burned in Ridgefield," Ben added. William had come limping home, safe but so tired that he slept for two days.

"They are evil men," Mother said, her lips set in a tight line.

"We gave them a good fight, though." Ben stopped his whittling, his eyes bright. "Our boys held off the British for fifteen minutes at Ridgefield. And General Arnold showed his bravery. His horse was shot out from under him. 'You are my prisoner!' shouted an enemy soldier. 'Not yet,' answered General Arnold, and he shot him dead. William saw it with his own eyes."

Father sighed. "It will take more than brave generals to win this war."

Hannah saw Ben pick up his knife, then put it down. His jaw was clenched tight.

"We will get back at the British for this," he said. "More men are joining the army every day. Daniel is going." He took a deep breath. "Father," he said, "I must go too."

Father stared at Ben. For a long moment neither of them spoke. The firelight danced on their serious faces. It was just the same as before, Hannah thought. No, this time something felt different.

"Please, Father," said Ben quietly, "give me your permission."

He was not angry, that was it. Just very sure.

Father answered just as quietly. "I will need to pray about it," he said.

Chapter 7

Cornmeal mush bubbled in the pot hanging over the fire. Bacon sizzled in the frying pan. Breakfast was almost ready.

But everything was so quiet. Hannah looked at Rebecca, busy slicing bread for toast. What was she thinking? She glanced over at Mother, stirring the kettle of mush so it wouldn't burn. She had hardly said a word this morning.

What had Father decided about Ben? Hannah was longing to ask, but she knew she couldn't. She had to wait for Father.

Tock-tock went the tall clock in the corner. *Tock-tock. Tock-tock.* Sometimes time flew by so fast. Like the dart of a hummingbird in

Mother's garden. And other times it crawled along so slowly that you could feel every single second.

Hannah went to get milk from the buttery next to the kitchen.

"What a morning!"

The door burst open, and Ben came stamping in from the barn. His shoes were muddy, and water streamed down his face. A cold, wet wind blew in with him. It was a stormy day, more like March than early May.

Father was just behind him. Quickly he closed the door. But it was opened again a minute later by Jemmy and Jonathan. They had been out scattering corn for the geese and chickens.

"You didn't throw it to them," Jonathan complained. "You just left it in a pile. How will they find it?"

"Those geese will find food wherever it is," Jemmy retorted.

Even Jemmy seemed quieter than usual today. Mother spread out all the wet clothes to dry near the fire. The smell of bacon mixed with damp wool as they sat down to eat.

Mother dished out bowls of hot cornmeal mush, and Rebecca passed the bacon. Spoons clinked against dishes. *Tock-tock* went the clock. Still no one spoke. They were all waiting, Hannah knew. Waiting for Father.

She stole a look at the end of the table. Father was eating just as slowly as he always did. He poured more molasses on his mush, and sprinkled maple sugar on top. He took a second piece of toast. He wiped his bowl with the crust. And then, finally, Father set down his spoon.

"Ben," he said, looking down the long table.

"Yes, sir." Ben sat soldier-straight in his chair. He seemed to be holding his breath.

"I have prayed long and hard on this matter. It is not easy to send a son off to war. Especially one so young." His voice caught, and he stopped. When he went on, his voice was steady. "But I know this war is just. Britain cannot rule us any longer. Her soldiers cannot be allowed to burn our towns. We must become a free nation. So I have decided that it is right for you to join the army."

"Oh, Father!" Ben cried joyfully. He started to jump up.

Father lifted his hand. "Wait," he said. "There is something else I want you to know. You recall that I had an older brother. The one you were named after."

Father had had three older brothers. Ben was the one who had died, Hannah remembered. Father never talked about him.

"My brother Ben was two years older than I was," Father went on. "We did everything together. We slept in the same bed, got up to feed the animals, and plowed the fields.

"Well, when my brother was eighteen, he took it into his head to go fight the French. He wanted to be a hero. So one day he ran off. Didn't even say good-bye, he was so afraid my father would stop him. After he left, we had one letter from him, and that was all. Six months later he was dead. He died out west somewhere, killed by Indians. My mother never got over that, Ben. She talked about him every day. And she read that letter over and over until it crumbled into dust in her hands. So you see, I hate war."

Hannah looked over at Mother. Her eyes were brimming with tears.

"That is why it has been so hard for me to give you my blessing," Father said. "Do you understand?"

Ben started to speak, but no words came out. He nodded.

"Well you have my blessing now."

Mother was crying quietly. Ben reached over to squeeze her hand.

It was Jemmy who broke the silence.

"When do you leave?" he asked eagerly. "Will you get into a battle right away? Are you taking Father's musket?"

Ben looked up. "Daniel is leaving in two days' time," he said. "I don't know about battles. Or Father's musket."

"You may take the musket," Father said. "It is my gift."

For the first time in weeks he and Ben smiled at each other.

"Two days' time," repeated Mother. "Oh, my. So soon?" She dabbed at her eyes with her handkerchief. Then suddenly she sat up straight. "You will need clothes. You have no summer shirts or stockings. And your breeches have been mended so many times." She shook her head. "We cannot send you marching off in rags."

"What can we do?" asked Hannah. There was no time to spin and weave and sew all that clothing.

"We will make Ben a suit of clothes fit for a soldier," Mother said.

"In just two days' time?" Rebecca looked doubtful too.

Mother stood up. Small as she was, she looked ready to lead an army.

"We can do it," she said.

Chapter 8

Suddenly time was racing by. *Tocktock, tock-tock, tocktock.* There was so much to do. And so few hours to get it done.

"A suit of clothes fit for a soldier." Somehow they had to spin the thread, weave the cloth, cut out and sew a shirt and breeches in just two days.

Like the general of her own little army, Mother set everyone to work.

Hannah was knitting. Making a pair of stockings that would have no holes. No strange lumps or bumps. These stockings were for Ben to march in, to fight in. They had to be perfect.

Rebecca was spinning faster than she ever

had before. She sat in the open doorway, the morning sun glinting in her hair. Her wheel hummed without stopping, turning the coarse flax into fine linen thread.

Mother was weaving. Upstairs in the back bedroom she took the thread and wound it onto spools called bobbins. These she fit into the shuttle, a boat-shaped piece of wood that she threw from side to side as she wove. *Thwack* went the loom. *Thwack. Thwack.* How many times? Hannah couldn't count. But each *thwack* was another row of thread added to the cloth that would become Ben's suit of clothes.

Even Jonathan was helping. He ran up and down stairs, fetching things. He brought more flax to Rebecca. He carried the spun thread up to Mother.

"I am making Ben's clothes too, aren't I?" he asked Hannah.

She stopped her knitting for a second to smile at him.

"You are," she said.

They worked, barely stopping for meals, until evening. Outside, Father and Ben and Jemmy were working just as hard. They finished the planting, and carried wood from the woodlot. They mended fences, and put everything in order in the barn. Jemmy would have to do all of Ben's work now.

"I can lift a fireplace log," he told Mother proudly. "And I'll chop all the wood you need for the kitchen fire."

"You are going to have so many extra chores," Father said. "Perhaps Hannah can help with the milking. And the sheep."

Did he mean it? Yes, Father always meant what he said. He was smiling at her. Ever since the night she had saved Smoke, he had looked at her in a different way. As if she could do things, just like the boys. Like Granny Hannah, Hannah thought.

"Oh, yes," she said happily.

The first stocking was finished. She showed it to Ben.

"Rebecca did a beautiful job," he said.

"Not Rebecca," Hannah protested. "I did it."

"You, Goosey?" He seemed puzzled.

"You knew it was me!"

His mouth turned up in that quick grin that she loved. It was that grin she was going to miss most, she realized.

"Of course I did," he said. "And you did a beautiful job. Thank you."

If Hannah kept working, maybe she could finish the second stocking tonight. Ben was mending a broken milk pail. Jemmy watched, as if trying to remember so he could do it next time. *Click, click. Tocktock.*

The stocking had to be perfect. She couldn't drop a stitch. Fit for a soldier, Hannah kept saying inside her head. But her eyelids were heavy. Her stitches were slowing down.

Then Mother was taking the stocking from her hands.

"Tomorrow is another day," she said softly.

———

Tomorrow came quickly. It was still dark outside when Hannah awoke. The first thing she thought of was Ben. One more day before he went marching off to become a soldier. One more day to finish his suit of clothes.

Hannah slipped out of bed, and went downstairs to poke up the kitchen fire.

But Mother was already there. The fire was blazing, and breakfast begun. She looked as if she had never gone to bed.

"One more day," she said, reading Hannah's thoughts. Her eyes looked tired and a little sad. But her jaw was set firm. Mother never gave up. "If we are to finish everything, we best get an early start."

By mid-morning Hannah had finished the second stocking. She laid it next to the first. It was exactly the same size, not longer or shorter as her stockings and mittens usually were. And no holes. Well, maybe just a tiny one near the toe. The stockings *were* fit for a soldier, she thought proudly.

Mother seemed to agree. Busy as she was, she stopped to squeeze Hannah's shoulder. "I couldn't have done better myself," she said, smiling.

But there was still much to be done. Mother hadn't yet started cutting out Ben's suit of clothes. And he must have two shirts, not just one, she'd decided.

"Hannah," she said, "do you think you could take over the spinning? Then Rebecca can work at the loom. And I can begin cutting and sewing."

No. That was Hannah's first thought. She was too clumsy. She could never spin as fast as Rebecca did. And Rebecca's thread was so smooth and fine. Hers would be poor.

But then she thought of Ben. Did it matter if she spun slowly, or if her thread was not so fine? What really mattered was that they finish Ben's suit of clothes today. If it would help for Hannah to spin, she had to do it.

"I will try," she said.

She took Rebecca's seat at the spinning wheel.

"Don't try too hard," Rebecca told her, putting the flax into her hands. "Just go slowly until you find the rhythm."

She disappeared up the stairs. *Thwack*, Hannah heard a moment later.

Jonathan was trotting around the room on his pretend horse, a long stick whose end Ben had carved to look like a horse's head.

"What is rhythm?" he stopped to ask.

Hannah thought for a minute. "It is the beat of music," she answered. "Like what you hear when the choir sings in church."

The beat of music. That was what her spinning needed to be.

She started the wheel moving with her right foot. It spun around, fast and even. Slow down, she thought.

Hannah wet her fingers in the water bowl. She held a strand of flax between them. Now, she told herself. Her foot rocked. Her fingers drew out the flax and smoothed it, then drew out more. Rebecca was right. There was a rhythm to it. She was beginning to feel it.

She glanced at her thread. Oh, no! It was twisting too tight.

Hannah sat still, blinking back tears. She was never going to get this right.

"Would you like to ride my horse?" Jonathan asked softly.

His eyes were so big in his small face. Hannah had to smile. "Not now," she said. "But thank you."

What had she been doing wrong? Slow down the wheel, she thought. Draw out the flax more quickly. She could do this. She had done the stockings, hadn't she? For Ben.

Once more she started her foot rocking.

Little by little it got easier. She felt the rocking, the drawing out, the smoothing, like the beat of music. She could almost hear music inside her head. Her fingers grew red and sore. But she kept on spinning.

"You're getting the feel of it," Rebecca said

when she came downstairs. "And your thread looks fine."

It wasn't really fine. Not like Rebecca's. But maybe it was good enough.

By late afternoon Mother was nearly finished with Ben's breeches. *Thwack* went the loom as Rebecca hurried to weave the cloth for his shirts. *Whirr* went the wheel as Hannah spun the thread for them.

Then, at last, they were finished with the spinning and weaving.

"Now you girls can help with the sewing," said Mother.

That night Mother lit the candles to give more light for sewing. Usually she thought the firelight was bright enough. This was Ben's last evening, Hannah thought, with a sinking feeling in her stomach.

All of them sat together around the huge stone fireplace. Ben, watched by Jemmy, was carving a new butter paddle for Mother. Jonathan sat at his feet, his dark head leaning on Ben's knee. Father was reading his Bible. Every once in a while he would read a verse out loud.

No one talked much. There was so much to say, and yet so little.

Mother's needle darted in and out, flashing in the firelight, making her tiny, perfect stitches. Hannah worked slowly on a sleeve, trying not to break her thread or tangle it.

The clock struck nine. Mother looked over at the boys.

"I'm not tired at all," protested Jonathan, though his eyes were closing.

Slowly, one by one, they trudged up the stairs to bed. It seemed hard to break away from the fireside this last evening. Ben was the last to go.

"You ought to get some rest," Mother told him. "For tomorrow."

Ben looked as if there was something he wanted to say. At that moment, Hannah thought, he didn't look like Ben, the big brother. Ben, the soldier. He looked like a little boy.

He swallowed hard. "Yes," was all he said.

But his hand touched the top of Hannah's head as he passed her chair.

The clock struck ten. And then, just a wink later, eleven. The fire was burning low. Father dozed in his chair, the Bible dropping from his hands. Still, Mother and Rebecca and Hannah kept sewing.

Tocktock, tocktock, tocktock. Almost time, said the clock.

Almost finished, thought Hannah.

The last thing was the collars. Mother let Rebecca and Hannah do the final stitching on them. Hannah's fingers were shaking, they were so tired and sore. But she forced them to hold the needle. Fit for a soldier, she told herself one more time.

She poked the needle into the soft linen. Oh so carefully she made tiny, even, perfect stitches. Nearly as tiny and even and perfect as Mother's.

There, she thought, as she did the very last

one. This is for you, Ben. And then, in a place inside where no one would see, she stitched one thing more. A tiny *H*.

The clock struck midnight. Hannah looked up. Rebecca had just finished too. Mother's face was so weary that it seemed she might never be able to move from her chair. But she was smiling.

"We did it," she whispered.

Chapter 9

Ben was dressed in his new suit of clothes. And everything fit just right. The breeches, the shirt, the stockings. He had new leather shoes made last winter. And Father's blue checked vest on top of his shirt.

Jonathan stared at him, blinking in the morning sun. "You look—" He stopped, trying to think of the right word.

"Splendid," said Mother softly.

"Splendid," repeated Jonathan. "Ben is splendid."

That was the right word, Hannah thought. Tall and strong, his cheeks scrubbed pink, he looked like he could win a war all by himself.

Mother fussed with his shirt. "Maybe we should have made the sleeves a little longer," she said. "You are still growing, you know."

Ben smiled at her. And at Rebecca and Hannah too. "The shirt is perfect," he said. "And so is everything else. Thank you all for working so hard."

Hannah hadn't told him about the little *H* she had stitched inside his collar. And she wouldn't, she decided. Maybe he would find it himself one day, and think of her.

"We will send more shirts," Mother told him. "And soon we will be starting to spin wool. The first thing we will make is a winter coat for you."

More spinning. Hannah would be helping, she knew. Maybe she would never like this kind of women's work as Mother did, or be able to spin as fine a thread as Rebecca. But she would be happy to be making a winter coat for Ben.

Right now there was one more thing she

could do for him. Help to cook his favorite dinner.

Since breakfast Mother had had the big iron pot going. Into the bubbling water she had put corned beef and salt pork. She was making a boiled dinner.

Hannah was in charge of the vegetables. She brought them up from the root cellar, and cut them in chunks. Then she sat watching the clock in the corner. Mother was very particular about when each one went into the pot.

At nine o'clock she dropped in the beets.

At exactly half-past ten she added the cabbage.

When the clock struck eleven, she put in the carrots and turnips.

At half-past eleven the parsnips and potatoes.

And fifteen minutes later the squash.

Hannah stirred the pot until everything was bubbling. In the meantime Mother and Rebecca had made a pudding and slid it into the oven to bake. Wonderful smells mixed together in the kitchen.

"Ahhh!" Ben sniffed loudly as he came in from the barn. The last time he would do that, Hannah thought. For how long? "It smells like a feast," he said.

And a feast it was. The biggest one since last Thanksgiving Day. Mother heaped the steaming meat onto a platter, with the vegetables all around it. There was bread and fresh-churned butter. Apple butter and pickles. Cider and sassafras tea. Around the table went the platter, again and again.

Father and Ben had three helpings each. Jemmy tried to keep up, but finally he had to put down his fork. "I feel like Mr. Spooner's hog," he said.

Mr. Spooner kept a hog that was the fattest in the county, everyone said.

"There is still bird's nest pudding to come," Mother told him.

With a grin, Jemmy picked up his spoon.

Rebecca dished out the pudding, made of apples in a sweet custard.

"Why is it called bird's nest pudding?" Jonathan wanted to know.

"See the currants in the center of each apple?" Hannah answered. "The apple is the nest and the currants are baby birds."

Jonathan smiled. "I like that," he said softly.

Hannah too felt as stuffed as Mr. Spooner's hog when the feast was finally over. Ben pushed back his chair and looked down the table at Mother.

"I don't know when I'll have another meal like this," he said.

Mother's eyes filled up with tears. Even Father had his handkerchief out, blowing his nose.

Jonathan looked at Ben with his big, serious eyes. "You can just come home," he said, "and we'll make you another one. Won't we, Hannah?"

Hannah swallowed hard. All she could do was nod her head.

Time rushed by so fast after that. Soon Daniel would be coming. Mother hurried to pack a supper for Ben to take with him. Jonathan begged for one last ride on Ben's back.

"Giddyap, horse!" he cried as they galloped around the house.

Then Ben disappeared upstairs. When he came down, he was holding something behind his back.

"This is for you," he said, handing Jemmy a small, carved wooden boat.

"It's just like the ships in the Connecticut navy!" Jemmy exclaimed.

For Jonathan there was a finely carved little horse. Of course, Hannah thought. This was what Ben had been whittling on the last few evenings.

And for Hannah, a lamb.

"Smoke!" she cried. It had just the look of her lamb, from the sweet face down to the funny little tail. She would keep it always. "Oh, Ben, thank you!"

And then, suddenly, Daniel was there, all dressed up and carrying his father's musket. Daniel wasn't nearly as tall as Ben. The gun barrel was almost as long as he was tall. He seemed hardly able to carry it. But his freckly face looked determined. Just like Ben.

"We best be going," Ben said quietly.

Father handed him the musket, newly oiled and shining. "Take good care of it, Son. And of yourself." That was all he said. But his hand tightly gripping Ben's seemed to be saying more. Father and Ben had made their peace, Hannah could see.

Ben hugged Mother, then Rebecca, and the rest of them in turn. He lifted the gun onto his shoulder. For a moment he stood in the doorway, looking at them. It was as if he were trying to memorize their faces.

"Write to us," said Mother, her voice almost a whisper.

"I will," promised Ben.

Then he turned. With Daniel beside him,

he marched off down the road in the spring sunshine. Off to be a soldier in General Washington's army.

Hannah stood by the front gate, watching him go. She felt as if her heart was breaking into tiny pieces.

"I will write to you!" she called.

Ben looked back, flashing her that special grin. "You do that, Goosey!"

"Every week!"

Once more he turned and waved. Hannah watched him, growing smaller and smaller in the distance. And then the road curved and Ben was gone.

Author's Note

Long ago, ships sailed from Europe, bringing families to settle the great wilderness that was America. The land was broken up into pieces called colonies. On the east coast, thirteen colonies belonged to England. But little by little, the people in these colonies became unhappy with the way they were treated by the English king. They thought the taxes they were asked to pay were unfair. They thought they should be allowed to make their own laws. Some even thought the colonies should break away from England and become a separate country.

On April 17, 1775, a large force of British soldiers met a small group of colonists at the village of Lexington, Massachusetts. Somehow, shots were fired and eight Americans were killed. The American Revolution had begun. Soon George Washington was chosen to lead the American army. And on July 4, 1776, men from all thirteen colonies met to sign a Declaration of Independence, telling England that they were now a free and independent country.

Before the war Fairfield, Connecticut, was one of the largest and richest towns in the colonies. It had a good harbor for shipping and good soil for farming. When the fighting began, young men from Fairfield marched off to Boston to help out. Farmers began growing extra grain, and women made tents, blankets, and clothing for the army. Then, in the summer of 1776, the war came much closer. The British army captured nearby New York City and Long Island.

Now the sails of enemy ships were often seen offshore. Small boats came across Long Island Sound in the dark of night to steal food and burn mills. Fairfield added more cannons to its small fort and more men to keep watch at night. But the British raids continued. In the spring of 1777, when Hannah's story takes place, Fairfield lived in constant fear of attack.

During the time of the Revolution, daily life was filled with hard work. Almost everything a family needed they made themselves. Along with any other job they might have, all the men were farmers. They raised corn and wheat for food, cows for milk and meat, sheep for wool, flax to spin into linen. The women kept a vegetable garden to feed the family. They made all the clothing, as well as soap, candles, butter, cheese, and other things needed in the house. The children helped with the chores, both inside and out in the fields.

Cooking in colonial times was much different than it is today. Preparing a meal could take hours. Most dinners were stews cooked in large iron pots over an open fire. Baking was done in brick ovens that had to be heated for several hours before the bread or pies could be put in. Still, the colonists made delicious foods. Here is a recipe for Bird's Nest Pudding that you can try. It has been changed to suit a modern kitchen. Be sure to have an adult help you.

3 T water	½ cup butter, softened
2 T flour	2 eggs
½ cup raisins	pinch of salt
4 firm apples, peeled, cored, and cut in half	⅛ tsp nutmeg
½ cup sugar	1 T melted butter

Preheat oven to 350°F. Mix flour and water to make a paste and brush on hollowed core of apples. Place raisins in paste on top of apples. Put apples in buttered nine-inch pie plate. Beat butter and sugar together. Add eggs (one at a time), salt, and nutmeg. Whip until light and fluffy. Pour mixture into a pot and heat very slowly on stove (if you heat too fast, eggs will scramble). Stir constantly until sugar dissolves and mixture is smooth and thick. Remove from heat and cool. Pour egg mixture around apples and brush with melted butter. Bake 45 minutes or until custard is just set. Makes 8 servings.

Acknowledgments

Almost all the names in this story are fictional. However, the Reverend Andrew Eliot actually existed, as did General Gold Selleck Silliman and General David Wooster. And the famous General Benedict Arnold really did fight in the raid on Danbury in April 1777.

My thanks to the many experts who shared their knowledge of colonial America and the Revolution with me, especially Barbara Austen, Librarian of the Fairfield Historical Society in Connecticut. I am also indebted to the Society for permission to adapt the recipe for Bird's Nest Pudding from their cookbook, *Cooking with Fire*. For help with the craft of spinning, I am grateful to Virginia M. Carnes of Muscoot Farm, and Althea Corey of Van Cortlandt Manor. And for their valuable advice on sheep, I thank Joe H. Plummer of Muscoot Farm, and Dana Meadows.

—J.V.L.

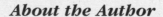

About the Author

Jean Van Leeuwen is the highly acclaimed author of many picture books and novels for young readers. Her previous works of Americana include the popular *Going West*; *Across the Wide Dark Sea*; and *Bound for Oregon*. She is also the author of *Two Girls in Sister Dresses*; *Blue Sky, Butterfly*; *Dear Mom, You're Ruining My Life*; and the best-selling Easy-to-Read books about Oliver and Amanda Pig. With the Pioneer Daughters series, Jean Van Leeuwen continues her tradition of stories that expand her readers' views of themselves and their world.